"I'm not following you. Where is he going to move to? London? Leonard has always told me how much he hates London."

"Not that he's actually been there more than a handful of times," Alessio returned drily. "But no. London wasn't what I had in mind."

"Then where?"

"I have a place at Lake Garda in northern Italy. It's close enough to get there on my private jet in a matter of hours so the trip shouldn't be too taxing for him."

"Oh, right. Okay."

"If we plan on leaving in roughly a week's time, it will give me sufficient time to get the ball rolling with the company so that I can install some of my own people to tie up all the loose ends. I'll also have enough time for my PA to source the best crew available to get this job done here and of course, there will have to be time spent packing away anything valuable that needs to be protected. I suggest several of the more robust rooms in the West Wing would be suitable for that."

"Wait, hang on just a minute! We...?"

Cathy Williams can remember reading Harlequin books as a teenager, and now that she is writing them, she remains an avid fan. For her, there is nothing like creating romantic stories and engaging plots, and each and every book is a new adventure. Cathy lives in London, and her three daughters—Charlotte, Olivia and Emma—have always been, and continue to be, the greatest inspirations in her life.

Books by Cathy Williams

Harlequin Presents

Desert King's Surprise Love-Child
Consequences of Their Wedding Charade
Hired by the Forbidden Italian
Bound by a Nine-Month Confession
A Week with the Forbidden Greek

Secrets of the Stowe Family

Forbidden Hawaiian Nights
Promoted to the Italian's Fiancée
Claiming His Cinderella Secretary

Visit the Author Profile page
at Harlequin.com for more titles.

Cathy Williams

—

THE HOUSEKEEPER'S INVITATION TO ITALY

HARLEQUIN®
PRESENTS™

Recycling programs
for this product may
not exist in your area.

ISBN-13: 978-1-335-58423-6

The Housekeeper's Invitation to Italy

Copyright © 2023 by Cathy Williams

Harlequin Enterprises ULC
22 Adelaide St. West, 41st Floor
Toronto, Ontario M5H 4E3, Canada
www.Harlequin.com

Printed in U.S.A.

THE HOUSEKEEPER'S INVITATION TO ITALY

CHAPTER ONE

THE BUILDING WASN'T quite what Sophie had been expecting. Although now that she was standing outside the impressive Georgian edifice she had to concede that she had just rushed to assume the obvious.

Arrogant billionaire…shiny over-the-top offices. The sort of place that announced in no uncertain terms that its occupant was not a man to be messed with because he was bigger, stronger and richer than you.

Buffeted by a brutal winter wind, and noting that it was already dark at a little after five-thirty in the afternoon, she remained hesitantly staring at the building.

It was an impeccably groomed four-storeyed town house, fronted by black railings and a shallow flight of steps that led up to a black door. In all respects it was identical to all the other town houses in this uber-prestigious crescent in the heart of London. From Bentleys to Teslas, every single car parked was high-end. There was a hush about the place which made her think that if she hung around for too long, staring and frowning and dithering, wondering whether she had done the right thing or not, then someone would materialise out of thin air and escort her right back to the busy streets a stone's throw away. Possibly by the scruff of her neck.

Galvanised by the prospect of that, Sophie hurried across the completely empty road, up the bank of steps, and realised that the gleaming brass knocker was just there for show—because there was a discreet panel of buttons to the side and a speakerphone.

Just for a few seconds, she took time out to contemplate where she was and why.

She'd had a long and uncomfortable journey from raw and wintry Yorkshire down to London—a journey undertaken with the sort of subterfuge she personally loathed, and with an outcome that was far from predictable. She had a message to be relayed under cover of darkness, because Leonard-White had expressly banned her from contacting his son, and what sort of reception was she going to get? Having gone against the wishes of her boss to uneasily follow what her inner voice had told her?

She had no idea, because Alessio Rossi-White, from everything she had seen of him, was a forbidding and terrifyingly remote law unto himself.

Sophie pressed the buzzer, and the nerves which she had been keeping at bay leapt out from their hiding places and her heart began to beat faster. The disembodied voice on the other end